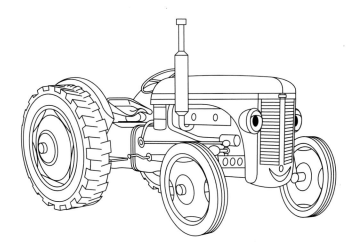

MR COOMBS THE GAMEKEEPER

One fine morning Fergus the little grey tractor and his friend Berty the Thirty were waiting in the barn for Farmer Pete.

They saw Mr Coombs the Gamekeeper coming into the farmyard. Mr Coombs was running and out of breath.

"Farmer Pete where are you?" He called, as he started to look around the farm buildings.

Farmer Pete was in the milking parlour cleaning up after the morning's milking.

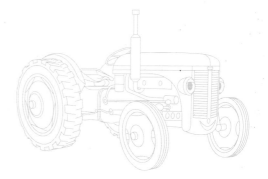

"Here I am Mr Coombs," answered Farmer Pete from the doorway of the milking parlour. "You look a bit hot, whatever is the matter?"

Mr Coombs stopped and took a deep breath, his face was shiny with sweat. He had obviously run a long way, as fast as he could.

"It's your cow number 74, she is up in the top field under the trees. She has just had her calf. The calf does not look well and cannot get up."

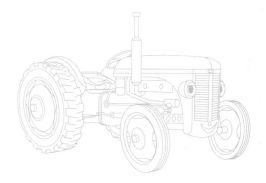

Farmer Pete stopped what he was doing, walked over to Fergus and said as he climbed into the seat, "Fergus old friend you have never let me down, please start first time. It is very important."

Farmer Pete turned the key. Ignition on, petrol on, push the lever and Fergus turned his engine. "Yes, yes, yes, yes, VROOM" and he was soon chuckling away.

"Well done Fergus, I knew I could rely on you," said Farmer Pete.

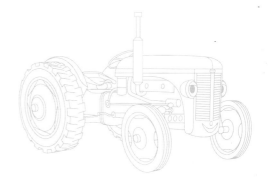

Farmer Pete drove Fergus across the farmyard and reversed him into the shed where he stored all the attachments.

He soon coupled him up to a transport box and drove back out into the yard.

"Hop in," shouted Farmer Pete to Mr Coombs the Gamekeeper. "It will be much easier riding in the transport box than running."

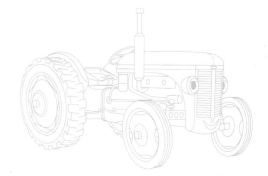

Farmer Pete and Mr Coombs were soon driving off along the track to where cow number 74 had last been seen with her newborn calf.

When they arrived at the top of the field, Farmer Pete drove Fergus along the edge of the wood looking for the new calf.

They soon found cow number 74. She was standing alongside her calf, licking it with her tongue, trying to get it to stand up.

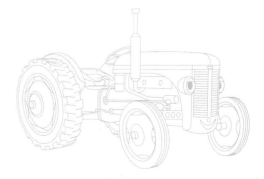

Farmer Pete drove Fergus in as close as he could to the newborn calf.

He got down from Fergus' seat and gently stroked cow number 74's nose.

He said, "come on now number 74, let us pick up your calf. We just need to carry it down to the farmyard so the Vet can check him over. You can walk behind Fergus and follow us back to the farmyard."

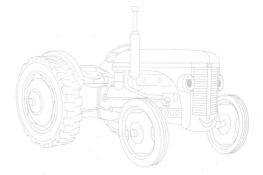

Mr Coombs sat in the transport box and Farmer Pete placed the calf across his lap. "Hold on tight to the calf Mr Coombs, it could be a bit of a bumpy ride," he said.

Farmer Pete climbed back into his seat and said, "nice and easy does it Fergus, we just need a slow journey. We don't want to lose Mr Coombs or the calf on the way, do we!"

Fergus set off back along the track very carefully, trying to avoid all of the bumps and holes.

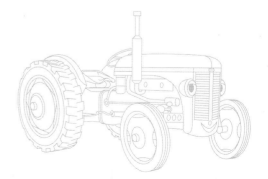

When they reached the farmyard, Farmer Pete drove straight to the pens where the young calves live until they are strong enough to go out into the fields. He stopped Fergus and opened the gate.

Suddenly, the calf jumped up and trotted off towards the other calves in the pen.

"It looks like he is going to be all right," said Mr Coombs. "Perhaps he was just lazy and did not want to walk back to the farmyard."

"You may be right, but I will still call the Vet, just to make sure he is fit and well," replied Farmer Pete.

"Thanks to Fergus and his transport box, bringing the calf back to the farmyard was easy," said Mr Coombs.

"A good job all around," said Farmer Pete. "If you hadn't seen the newborn calf Mr Coombs, it could have become ill and we may have lost him. With the help of 'Fergus the animal ambulance', I think we can say that today we saved a life."

Fergus sat in the yard smiling to himself. He was very proud of how he had helped save the newborn calf.

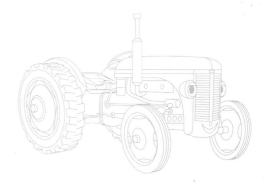

"With all of this excitement I feel quite thirsty," said Farmer Pete, "how about a nice cup of tea Mr Coombs?"

"Thank you very much Farmer Pete, I would love one," said Mr Coombs, who rarely said no to a cup of tea.

While the Vet was checking the calf, Farmer Pete and Mr Coombs sat on the hay trailer enjoying their tea in the sunshine.

When the Vet returned from the pens he announced that the calf was healthy and should grow into a fine animal.

After Mr Coombs and the Vet had left, Farmer Pete put Fergus back into the barn alongside Berty.

"Sleep well tonight old friend," he said. "You have earned your rest today. It was very important that we saved that young calf and it would have been difficult without you." He patted Fergus on the bonnet and closed the barn doors behind him.

Fergus told the story to Berty the Thirty and as soon as the story was over they both closed their eyes and went to sleep, dreaming of wonderful new adventures.

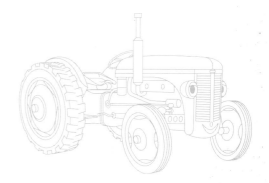

FERGUS' STORY   MR COOMBS THE GAMEKEEPER   GEOF
THE MECHANIC   FERGUS GETS A NEW FRIEND   NEVILL
GETS HIS NAME   NEVILLE AND THE HOT AIR BALLOO
FERGUS' BONFIRE NIGHT   FERGUS AT THE BARN FIR
FERGUS AND BERTY CLEAR THE SNOW   FERGUS' CHRISTMA
SPECIAL   THE SPRING TIME SURPRISE   FERGUS AND TH
NEW BUILDING   FERGUS' HALLOWEEN   FERGUS AND TH
STEAM UP   FERGUS AND BERTY GO POTATO PLANTIN
FERGUS AND THE BEAVER SCOUTS   THE WEDDING DA
FERGUS AND THE FLOOD   FERGUS AT THE CIRCUS   FERGU
AND THE HEATWAVE   FERGUS AT THE CARNIVAL   FERGU
AT THE PLOUGHING MATCH   FERGUS AND THE FALLEN TRE

FERGUS' STORY   MR COOMBS THE GAMEKEEPER   GEOF
THE MECHANIC   FERGUS GETS A NEW FRIEND   NEVILL
GETS HIS NAME   NEVILLE AND THE HOT AIR BALLOO
FERGUS' BONFIRE NIGHT   FERGUS AT THE BARN FIR
FERGUS AND BERTY CLEAR THE SNOW   FERGUS' CHRISTMA